MAD ABOUT
MADELINE

MAD ABOUT
MADELINE

THE COMPLETE TALES

LUDWIG BEMELMANS

VIKING

VIKING
Published by the Penguin Group
Penguin Putnam Books for Young Readers, 345 Hudson Street, New York, New York 10014, U.S.A.
Penguin Books Ltd, 27 Wrights Lane, London W8 5TZ, England
Penguin Books Australia Ltd, Ringwood, Victoria, Australia
Penguin Books Canada Ltd, 10 Alcorn Avenue, Toronto, Ontario, Canada M4V 3B2
Penguin Books (N.Z.) Ltd, 182-190 Wairau Road, Auckland 10, New Zealand

Penguin Books Ltd, Registered Offices: Harmondsworth, Middlesex, England

First published by Viking, a division of Penguin Books USA Inc., 1993
This edition published by Viking, a division of Penguin Putnam Books for Young Readers, 2001

1 3 5 7 9 10 8 6 4 2

The Library of Congress has cataloged the 1993 edition as follows:
Bemelmans, Ludwig, 1898-1962.
[Selections]
Mad about Madeline : the collected tales / story and pictures by Ludwig Bemelmans.
p. cm.
Contents: Madeline—Madeline's rescue—Madeline and the bad hat—Madeline and the gypsies—
Madeline in London—Madeline's Christmas.
ISBN 0-670-85187-6 (set)
1. Children's stories, American. [1. Paris (France)—Fiction. 2. Boarding schools—Fiction.
3. Schools—Fiction. 4. Stories in rhyme.] I. Title.
PZ8.3.B425Maac 1993 [E]—dc20 93-14663 CIP AC

This edition ISBN 0-670-88816-8

Printed in U.S.A
Set in Bodoni

CONTENTS

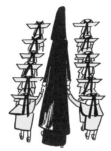

With a selection of original sketches of Madeline
from Ludwig Bemelmans' notebooks

Introduction

During the years that our three children were growing from babyhood to youth, *Madeline* was not considered as much a book in our household as it was a language and a way of life. When Maria, our youngest, broke her arm and her brothers were grousing about the tucking up on the sofa and the public allure of her fuchsia cast, it seemed perfectly natural to turn to them and say, "Boohoo, we want to have our arms broken, too."

When I was trying to describe Maria's character to a friend long distance, I finally resorted to the simplest way of evoking little girl feistiness: "To the tiger in the zoo / Madeline just said, 'Pooh-pooh.'" And occasionally all three of my children must tire of my tendency to move through their rooms from time to time in the dark moments after the light has just been turned off, saying softly, "'Goodnight little girls! / Thank the lord you are well! / And now go to sleep!' / said Miss Clavel."

I can recite *Madeline* by heart, as my children know well. But it's likely that, in small chunks, they can recite it, too. In fact, it would not be too much of a stretch to say that most of the people I know know *Madeline* by heart.

This is curious. Amid a childhood full of children's books, amid glorious pictures and imaginative plots, it is worth wondering why this story is among a handful of books that now-grown children can declaim without a text, that now-grown children invariably buy for their own more than half a century after Ludwig Bemelmans began writing it on the back of a restaurant menu.

Why would three American children who go to a day school, have never visited Paris or worn a uniform, and who are still flummoxed by why Miss Clavel wears a veil be almost instantly and consistently en rapport with twelve little girls in two straight lines being led by their boarding school nurse in flat sailor hats and identical coats through the Place de la Concorde and past Notre Dame?

The answer, I think, can be contained in one word: attitude. And the attitude, of course, belongs to Madeline, "the smallest one." Through the other books—

Madeline's Rescue, Madeline's Christmas, Madeline and the Gypsies, Madeline and the Bad Hat, Madeline in London—we never even learn the names of the eleven other girls, who are barely discernable from one another except for variations of hair.

But we know of Madeline all we need to know of anyone's character: that she is utterly fearless and sure of herself, small in stature but large in moxie. Not afraid of mice, of ice, or of teetering on a stone bridge over a river. It's a mistake to stretch childhood associations too far—and also a mistake not to take them seriously enough—but it would not be stretching it too far to say that, for little girls especially, Madeline is a kind of role model. That "pooh-pooh" rang enduringly in the ears of many of us. Translation from the French: Stand back, world. I fear nothing.

The role of gutsy girls in children's literature should never be discounted, from Anne Shirley of the Green Gables series to Jo March in *Little Women*. When I was a girl, girl characters who were outspoken, smart, strong, and just a bit disobedient were the primary way I found to define and discover myself and all the ways in which I felt different from standard notions of femininity.

But for younger children, the girls in storybooks have, until recently, most often been princesses spinning straw into gold or sleeping their lives away until a prince plants the kiss of true love on their compliant lips. Perhaps the best-known exception is Kay Thompson's Eloise, a little girl with untidy hair and manners who lives—and writes on the walls—in the Plaza Hotel.

Truth to tell, I have always found Eloise's chaotic existence and her self-protective little asides about her mother shopping at Bergdorf's a bit pathetic and lonely, a decidedly grown-up version of the madcap child. When I think of Eloise grown up, I think of her with a drinking problem, knocking about from avocation to avocation, unhappily married or unhappily divorced, childless.

When I think of Madeline grown up, I think of her as the French Minister of Culture or the owner of a stupendous couture house, sending her children off to Miss Clavel to be educated. Perhaps they have apprehended all this, but while my children like Eloise, they *live* Madeline, which makes all the difference.

For those of us who believe that children feel secure with structure, part of the enduring charm of the books surely must be that Madeline's confidence and fearlessness are set within a backdrop of utter safety. While Eloise's nanny, for instance, is always at her wit's end, Miss Clavel is concerned but competent, and life is safe within the "old house in Paris / that was covered with vines."

In their two straight lines the children march predictably through life, with Madeline the admired wild card who reforms the rambunctious Bad Hat and runs away with the gypsies. Even when she has what has become the best-known emergency appendectomy in literature, the surgery becomes simultaneously an adventure and a school routine, the kind of combination of the scary and the safe that is alluring when you are trying to become yourself.

It's a combination of the masterly and the simplistic that makes the drawings so successful, too. I hope it would not offend Bemelmans to say that the illustrations are in many ways quite childlike: the simply, almost crude lines of the interiors; the faces with dot eyes and U-shaped mouths; the scribble quality to much of the detail work. The rendering of the Eiffel Tower as a Christmas tree in the holiday Madeline book is wonderful and yet sensible to children, who might well embellish the landmark in exactly the same way.

Rich picture books are wonderful, but when you are little they often make you feel rather incompetent. Madeline is different. Of course the simplicity of the drawings is quite deceptive; the one in which Madeline stands on the bed and shows the other girls her scar after the appendectomy is perhaps as good a rendering of carriage-as-character as I've ever seen outside of Holbein's portraits. But the best children's illustrators have a good deal of child in them, and Bemelmans is no exception. "He colors outside the lines," my oldest child said approvingly.

Classics are always ineffable: why does *Goodnight Moon* appeal for generation after generation, despite changes in mores, manners, technology, and television fare? Why do children as different as Abbott and Costello agree completely about the indispensability of *The Cat in the Hat*? Why does *A Wrinkle in Time* speak as clearly to my sons as it did to me three decades ago? What is it that Sendak has that lesser lights just do not?

The answer, I think, is that there are certain books written out of some grown-up's idea of children, of who they are and what they should be like, of what we like to think absorbs and amuses them. And then there are the books that are written for real children by people who manage, however they do it, to maintain an utterly childlike part of their minds. They understand that children prize security and adventure, both bad behavior and conformity, both connections and independence.

Madeline charms because of rhyme and meter, vivid illustrations and engaging situations. But the Madeline books endure because they understand children and epitomize what they fear, what they desire, and what they hope to be, in the person of one little girl. A risk taker. An adventurer. And at the end, a small child drifting off to sleep. "That's all there is— / there isn't any more."

Anna Quindlen
November 1993

MADELINE

In an old house in Paris

that was covered with vines

lived twelve little girls in two straight lines.

In two straight lines they broke their bread

and brushed their teeth

and went to bed.

They smiled at the good

and frowned at the bad

and sometimes they were very sad.

They left the house

at half past nine

in two straight lines

in rain

or shine—

the smallest one was Madeline.

She was not afraid of mice—

she loved winter, snow, and ice.

To the tiger in the zoo

Madeline just said, "Pooh-pooh,"

and nobody knew so well
how to frighten Miss Clavel.

In the middle of one night
Miss Clavel turned on her light
and said, "Something is not right!"

Little Madeline sat in bed,
cried and cried; her eyes were red.

And soon after Dr. Cohn

came, he rushed out to the phone

and he dialed: DANton-ten-six—

"Nurse," he said, "it's an appendix!"

Everybody had to cry—

not a single eye was dry.

Madeline was in his arm

in a blanket safe and warm.

In a car with a red light

they drove out into the night.

Madeline woke up two hours
later, in a room with flowers.

Madeline soon ate and drank.

On her bed there was a crank,

and a crack on the ceiling had the habit
of sometimes looking like a rabbit.

Outside were birds, trees, and sky—
and so ten days passed quickly by.

One nice morning Miss Clavel said—

"Isn't this a fine—

day to visit

Madeline."

VISITORS FROM TWO TO FOUR

read a sign outside her door.

Tiptoeing with solemn face,

with some flowers and a vase,

in they walked and then said, "Ahhh,"
when they saw the toys and candy
and the dollhouse from Papa.

But the biggest surprise by far—
on her stomach
was a scar!

"Good-by," they said, "we'll come again,"

and the little girls left in the rain.

They went home and broke their bread

brushed their teeth

and went to bed.

In the middle of the night
Miss Clavel turned on the light
and said, "Something is not right!"

And afraid of a disaster

Miss Clavel ran fast

and faster,

and she said, "Please children do—
tell me what is troubling you?"

And all the little girls cried, "Boohoo,
we want to have our appendix out, too!"

"Good night little girls!
Thank the lord you are well!
And now go to sleep!"
said Miss Clavel.

And she turned out the light—

and closed the door—

and that's all there is—

there isn't any more.

HERE is a list for those who may wish to identify the Paris scenes Ludwig Bemelmans has pictured in this book.

On the cover and in one of the
illustrations
THE EIFFEL TOWER

In the picture of the lady feeding
the horse
THE OPERA

A gendarme chases a jewel thief across
THE PLACE VENDOME

A wounded soldier at
THE HOTEL DES INVALIDES

A rainy day in front of
NOTRE DAME

A sunny day looking across
THE GARDEN AT THE LUXEMBOURG

Behind the little girls skating is
THE CHURCH OF THE SACRE COEUR

A man is feeding birds in
THE TUILERIES GARDENS FACING
THE LOUVRE

MADELINE'S RESCUE

MADELINE'S
RESCUE

In an old house in Paris that was covered with vines

Lived twelve little girls in two straight lines.

They left the house at half past nine

In two straight lines in rain or shine.

The smallest one was Madeline.

She was not afraid of mice.

She loved the winter, snow, and ice.

To the tiger in the zoo

Madeline just said, "Pooh pooh!"

And nobody knew so well

How to frighten Miss Clavel—

Until the day she slipped and fell.

Poor Madeline would now be dead

But for a dog

That kept its head,

And dragged her safe from a watery grave.

"From now on, I hope you will listen to me,

"And here is a cup of camomile tea.

"Good night, little girls—I hope you sleep well."

"Good night, good night, dear Miss Clavel!"

Miss Clavel turned out the light.

After she left there was a fight

About where the dog should sleep that night.

The new pupil was ever
So helpful and clever.

The dog loved biscuits, milk, and beef

And they named it Genevieve.

She could sing and almost talk

And enjoyed the daily walk.

Soon the snow began to fly,

Inside it was warm and dry

And six months passed quickly by.

When the first of May came near

There was nervousness each year.

For on that day arrived a collection

Of trustees for the annual inspection.

The inspection was most thorough,

Much to everybody's sorrow.

"Tap, tap!" "Whatever can that be?"

"Tap, tap!" "Come out and let me see!

"Dear me, it's a dog! Isn't there a rule

"That says DOGS AREN'T ALLOWED IN SCHOOL?"

"Miss Clavel, get rid of it, please,"

Said the president of the board of trustees.

"Yes, but the children love her so,"

Said Miss Clavel. "Please don't make her go."

"I daresay," said Lord Cucuface.

"I mean—it's a perfect disgrace

"For young ladies to embrace

"This creature of uncertain race!

"Off with you! Go on—run! scat!

"Go away and don't come back!"

Madeline jumped on a chair.

"Lord Cucuface," she cried, "beware!"

"Miss Genevieve, noblest dog in France,

"You shall have your VEN-GE-ANCE!"

"It's no use crying or talking.

"Let's get dressed and go out walking.

"The sooner we're ready, the sooner we'll leave—

"The sooner we'll find Miss Genevieve."

They went looking high

and low

And every place a dog might go.

In every place they called her name

But no one answered to the same.

The gendarmes said, "We don't believe

"We've seen a dog like Genevieve."

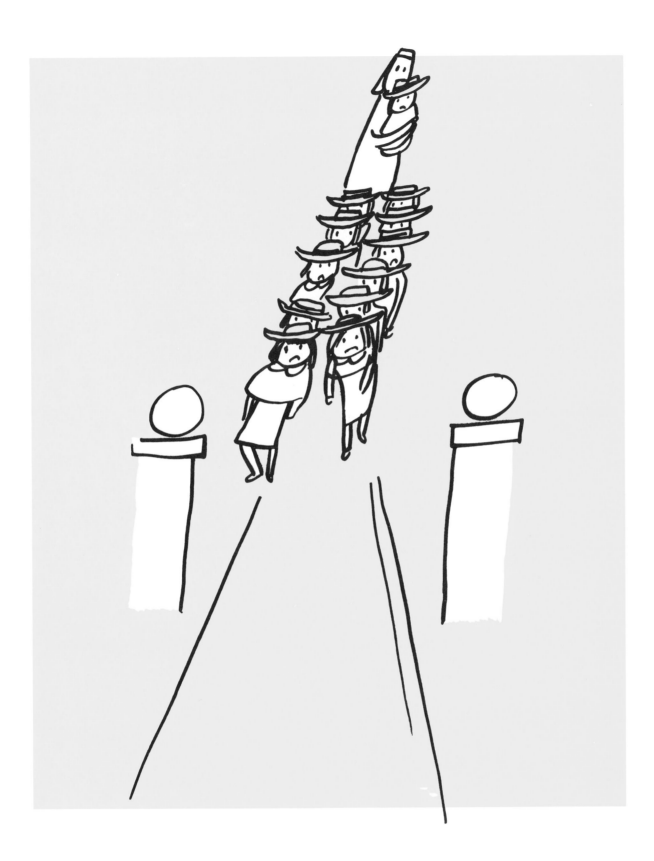

Hours after they had started
They came back home broken-hearted.

"Oh, Genevieve, where can you be?

"Genevieve, please come back to me."

In the middle of the night
Miss Clavel turned on the light.
And said, "Something is not right."

An old street lamp shed its light
On Miss Genevieve outside.

She was petted, she was fed,

And everybody went to bed.

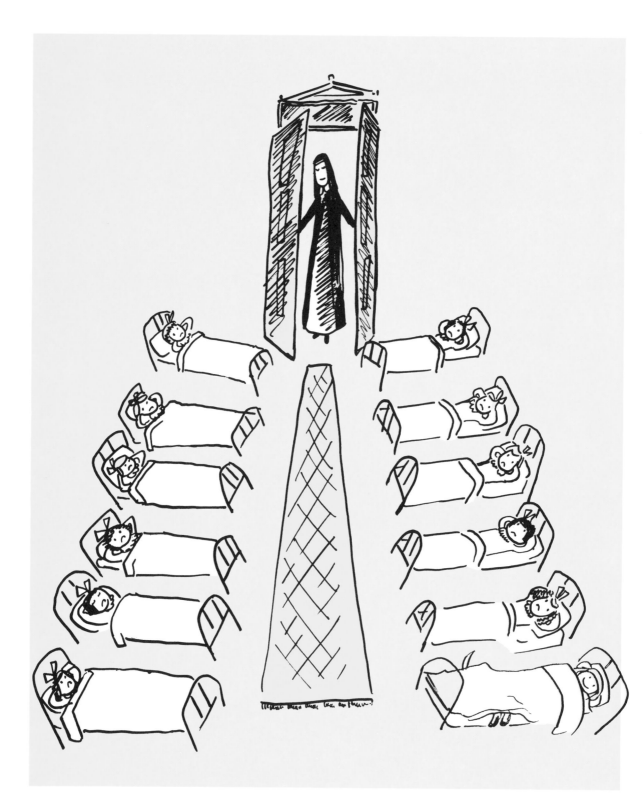

"Good night, little girls, I hope you sleep well."

"Good night, good night, dear Miss Clavel!"

Miss Clavel turned out the light,

And again there was a fight,

As each little girl cried,

"Genevieve is *mine* tonight!"

For a second time that night

Miss Clavel turned on her light,

And afraid of a disaster,
She ran fast—

And even faster.

"If there's one more fight about Genevieve,

"I'm sorry, but she'll have to leave!"

That was the end of the riot—
Suddenly all was quiet.

For the third time that night
Miss Clavel turned on the light,

And to her surprise she found

That suddenly there was enough hound

THE END

To go all around.

MADELINE AND THE BAD HAT

To
Mimi

In an old house in Paris
That was covered with vines
Lived twelve little girls
In two straight lines.
They left the house at half-past-nine
In two straight lines, in rain or shine.
The smallest one was Madeline.

One day the Spanish Ambassador

Moved into the house next door.

Look, my darlings, what bliss, what joy!

His Excellency has a boy.

Madeline said, "It is evident that
This little boy is a Bad Hat!"

In the spring when birdies sing

Something suddenly went "zing!"

Causing pain and shocked surprise
During morning exercise.

On hot summer nights he ghosted;

In the autumn wind he boasted

That he flew the highest kite.

Year in, year out, he was polite.

He was sure and quick on ice,

And Miss Clavel said, "Isn't he nice!"

One day he climbed upon the wall
And cried, "Come, I invite you all!
Come over some time, and I'll let you see
My toys and my menagerie—
My frogs and birds and bugs and bats,
Squirrels, hedgehogs, and two cats.
The hunting in this neighborhood
Is exceptionally good."

But Madeline said, "Please don't molest us,
Your menagerie does not interest us."

He changed his clothes and said, "I bet
This invitation they'll accept."

Madeline answered, "A Torero

Is not at all our idea of a hero!"

The poor lad left; he was lonesome and blue;

He shut himself in—what else could he do?

But in a short while, the little elf
Was back again, and his old self.

Said Miss Clavel, "It seems to me

He needs an outlet for his energy.

"A chest of tools might be attractive

For a little boy that's very active.

"I knew it—listen to him play,

Hammering, sawing, and working away."

Oh, but that boy was really mean!

He built himself a GUILLOTINE!

He was unmoved by the last look

The frightened chickens gave the cook.

He ate them ROASTED, GRILLED, and FRITO!

¡Oh, what a horror was PEPITO!

One day, when out to take the air,

Madeline said, "Oh, look who's there!"

Pepito carried a bulging sack.

He was followed by an increasing pack

Of all the dogs in the neighborhood.

"That boy is simply misunderstood.

Look at him bringing those doggies food!"

He said, "Let's have a game of tag"—
And let a CAT out of the bag!

There were no trees, and so instead
The cat jumped on Pepito's head.

And now just listen to the poor

Boy crying, "AU SECOURS!"

Which you must cry, if by chance

You're ever in need of help in France.

Miss Clavel ran fast and faster

To the scene of the disaster.

She came in time to save the Bad Hat,

And Madeline took care of the cat.

Good-by, Fido; so long, Rover.

Let's go home—the fun is over.

There was sorrowing and pain

In the Embassy of Spain.

The Ambassadress wept tears of joy,

As she thanked Miss Clavel for saving her boy.

"Nothing," said the Ambassador,

"Would cheer up poor Pepito more

Than a visit from next door.

"Only one visitor at a time,

Will you go in first, Miss Madeline?"

So Madeline went in on tiptoe,

And whispered, "Can you hear me, Pepito?

It serves you right, you horrid brat,

For what you did to that poor cat."

"I'll never hurt another cat,"
Pepito said. "I swear to that.
I've learned my lesson. Please believe
I'm turning over a new leaf."
"That's fine," she said. "I hope you do.
We all will keep our eyes on you!"

And lo and behold, the former Barbarian

Turned into a Vegetarian.

And the starling and turtle, the bunny and bat,

Went back to their native habitat.

His love of animals was such,

Even Miss Clavel said,

"It's too much!"

The little girls all cried "Boo-hoo!"

But Madeline said, "I know what to do."

And Madeline told Pepito that
He was no longer a BAD HAT.
She said, "You are our pride and joy,
You are the world's most wonderful boy!"

They went home and broke their bread
And brushed their teeth and went to bed,

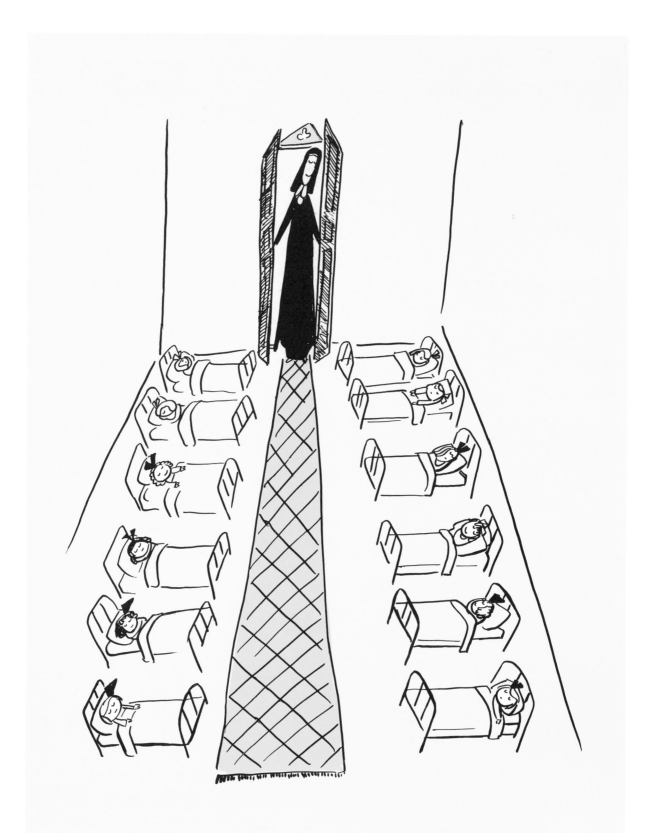

And as Miss Clavel turned out the light
She said, "I knew it would all come out right."

MADELINE AND THE GYPSIES

MADELINE and the
GYPSIES

In an old house in Paris that was
    covered with vines
Lived twelve little girls in two
    straight lines.
In two straight lines they broke
    their bread
And brushed their teeth and went
    to bed.
They left the house at half-past
    nine—
The smallest one was Madeline.
In another old house that stood
    next door
Lived the son of the Spanish
    Ambassador.
He was all alone; his parents were
    away;
He had no one with whom to play.
He asked, "Please come, I invite
    you all,
To a wonderful Gypsy Carnival."
And so—
        Dear reader—

Here we go!

Up and down and down and up—
They hoped the wheel would never stop.
Round and round; the children cried,
"Dear Miss Clavel, just one more ride!"

A sudden gust of wind,

A bolt of lightning,

Even the Rooster found it frightening.

The big wheel stops; the passengers land.

How fortunate there is a taxi stand!

"Hurry, children, off with these things!

You'll eat in bed."

Mrs. Murphy brings

The soup of the evening; it is half-past nine.

"Good heavens, where is MADELINE?"

Poor Miss Clavel, how would she feel
If she knew that on top of the Ferris wheel,
In weather that turned from bad to rotten,
Pepito and Madeline had been forgotten?

Pepito said, "Don't be afraid.
I will climb down and get some aid."
It was downpouring more and more
As he knocked on the Gypsies' caravan door.

The Gypsy Mama with her umbrella went
And got some help in the circus tent.
With the aid of the strong man and the clown,
Madeline was safely taken down.

The Gypsy Mama tucked them in
And gave them potent medicine.

The big wheel was folded, and the tent.

They packed their wagons and away they went.

For Gypsies do not like to stay—

They only come to go away.

A bright new day—the sky is blue;

The storm is gone; the world is new.

This is the Castle of Fountainblue—

"All this, dear children, belongs to you."

How wonderful to float in a pool,

Watch other children go to school,

Never to have to brush your teeth,

And never—never—

To go to sleep.

The Gypsies taught them grace

And speed,

And how to ride

The circus steed.

Then Madeline said, "It's about time
We sent dear Miss Clavel a line."

Poor Miss Clavel—a shadow of her former self

From worrying, because, instead of twelve,

There were only eleven little girls—

Stopped brushing their curls

    And suddenly revived

    When the postal card arrived.

"Thank heaven," she said, "the children are well!

But dear, oh dear, they've forgotten how to spell."

She studied the postmark, and then fast and faster

They rushed to the scene of the disaster.

The Gypsy Mama didn't like at all
What she saw in her magic crystal ball.

The Gypsy Mama said, "How would you like to try on
This lovely costume of a lion?"

With a curved needle and some string

She sewed both the children in,

And nobody knew what was inside

The tough old lion's leathery hide.

This was a fascinating game.

Compared to this, all else was tame.

A circus lion earns his bread

By scaring people half to death.

And after doing that, he's fed.

And after that, he's put to bed.

A lovely dawn and all was well;

The lion roamed through wood and dell.

He smelled sweet flowers; he came to a farm;

He frightened the barnyard—

Intending no harm.

They saw a man and said, "Please help
Us to get out of this old pelt."

The man was a hunter; he took his gun;

He got to his feet and started to run.

Said the lion, "We'd better go back, for if we're not
In a zoo or circus, we'll surely be shot."

They got to the tent
In time for the show.

"Look," said Madeline,

"There in the first row—"

"Oh yes," said Pepito,

"There are people we know!"

"Dear Miss Clavel! At last we found you!
Please let us put our arms around you."

The Gypsy Mama sobbed her grief
Into her only handkerchief.

The strong man suddenly felt weak,

And tears were running down his cheek.

Even the poor clown had to cry

As the time came to say good-bye.

The best part of a voyage—by plane,

By ship,

Or train—

Is when the trip is over and you are

Home again.

Here is a freshly laundered shirty—

It's better to be clean than dirty.

In two straight lines
They broke their bread
And brushed their teeth
And went to bed.

"Good night, little girls, thank the Lord you are well!

And now PLEASE go to sleep," said Miss Clavel.

And she turned out the light and closed the door—

And then she came back, just to count them once more!

Scenery in

MADELINE
and the Gypsies

MADELINE IN LONDON

In an old house
in Paris

that was covered
with vines

Lived twelve little girls
in two straight lines.

They left the house

at half past nine.

The smallest one
was Madeline.

In another old house
that stood next door

Lived Pepito,
the son of

the Spanish Ambassador.

An Ambassador doesn't
have to pay rent,
But he has to move
to wherever he's sent.

He took his family
and his hat;

They left for England—
all but the cat.

"I'm glad," said the cat.

"There goes that bad hat.

Let him annoy some other kitten

At the Embassy in Great Britain."

The little girls all cried: "Boo-hoo—

We'd like to go to London too."

In London Pepito picked at his dinner,
Soon he grew thin and then he grew thinner—

And when he began to look like a stick
His mama said, "My, this boy looks sick.
I think Pepito is lonely for
Madeline and the little girls next door."

His papa called Paris. "Hello, Miss Clavel,
My little Pepito is not at all well.

"He misses you; and he's lonesome for
Madeline and the little girls next door.

"May we request the pleasure of your company—
There's plenty of room here at our embassy."

"Quick, darlings, pack your bags, and we'll get
Out to the airport and catch the next jet."

Fill the house with lovely flowers,

Fly our flags from all the towers.

For Pepito's birthday bake
The most wonderful birthday cake.

Place twelve beds in two straight lines.
The last one here will be Madeline's.

"Welcome to London, the weather's fine,
And it's exactly half past nine."

"Good Heavens," said Miss Clavel, "we've brought no toy

For his excellency's little boy!"

Said Madeline, "Everybody knows, of course,

He always said he craved a horse."

In their little purses and in Miss Clavel's bag

There wasn't enough money to buy the meanest nag.

But in London there's a place to get

A retired horse to keep as a pet.

And when they went to the place, they found
A horse that was gentle, strong, and sound.

Some poor old dobbins are made into glue,

But not this one—

Look, he's as good as new.

"Happy birthday, Pepito, happy birthday to you.

This lovely horse belongs to you."

Just then— "Tara, tara"—a trumpet blew
Suddenly outside, and off he flew
Over the wall to take his place at the head

Of the Queen's Life Guards, which he had always led
Before the Royal Society for the Protection of Horses
Had retired him from Her Majesty's Forces.

"Oh, dear! They've gone. Oh, what a pity!

Come, children, we'll find them in the city."

"Careful, girls, watch your feet.

Look right before you cross the street."

Oh, for a cup of tea and crumpets—

Hark, hark, there goes the sound of trumpets.

These birds have seen

all this before.

But they are glad

of an encore.

And so are the people—on ship . . .

and shore.

And now it's getting really grand.

Here comes the mascot and his band.

The people below are stout and loyal,

And those on the balcony mostly Royal.

The show is over, it's getting dark

In the city, in the park.

Dinner is waiting; we must be on time.

Now let's find Pepito and Madeline.

Well, isn't is lovely—they're standing sentry

Right here at the Whitehall entry.

That is the power and the beauty:

In England everyone does his duty!

Visiting is fun and gay—

Let's celebrate a lovely day.

Everyone had been well fed,

Everyone was in his bed.

Only one was forgotten, he'd been on his feet
All day long, without anything to eat.

In a cottage that was thatched,

Wearing trousers that were patched,

Lived a gardener, who loved flowers,

Especially in the morning hours,

When their faces, fresh with dew,

Smiled at him—"How DO you do?"

The gardener, who was never late,

Opened up the garden gate.

The gardener dropped his garden hose.

There wasn't a daisy or a rose.

"All my work and all my care
For nought! Oh, this is hard to bear.

"Where's my celery, carrots, tomatoes, my beans and peas?
And not an apple on my apple trees!"

Everybody had to cry.

Not a single eye was dry.

Oh, look who is lying there,

With his feet up in the air.

"I feel his breath, he's not dead yet.

Quick, Pepito, get the vet."

The vet said, "Don't worry, he's only asleep.

Help me get him on his feet.

"As a diet, there is nothing worse

Than green apples and roses for an old horse."

"Dear lady," said Miss Clavel, "we beg your pardon.

It seems our horse has eaten up your garden.

"A little sunshine, a little rain,

And it all will be the same again."

Pepito's mother said, "Quite so, quite so!

Still I'm afraid the horse must go."

Then Madeline cried, "I know what to do.
Pepito, let us take care of him for you."

"Fasten your seat belts, in half an hour
You will see the Eiffel Tower."

"Madeline, Madeline, where have you been?"

"We've been to London to see the Queen."

"At last," sighed Madeline, "we are able
To sit down without being thirteen at table."

They brushed his teeth and gave him bread,

And covered him up

and put him to bed.

"Good night, little girls,

Thank the Lord you are well.

And now go to sleep," said Miss Clavel.

And she turned out the light and closed the door.

There were twelve upstairs, and below one more.

MADELINE'S CHRISTMAS

MADELINE'S CHRISTMAS

In an old house in Paris

That was covered with vines

Lived twelve little girls

In two straight lines.

They left the house at half-past nine

In two straight lines, in rain or shine.

The smallest one was MADELINE.

She was not afraid of mice

she loved winter, snow and ice

And to the tiger in the zoo

Madeline just said . . .

"POOH, POOH!"

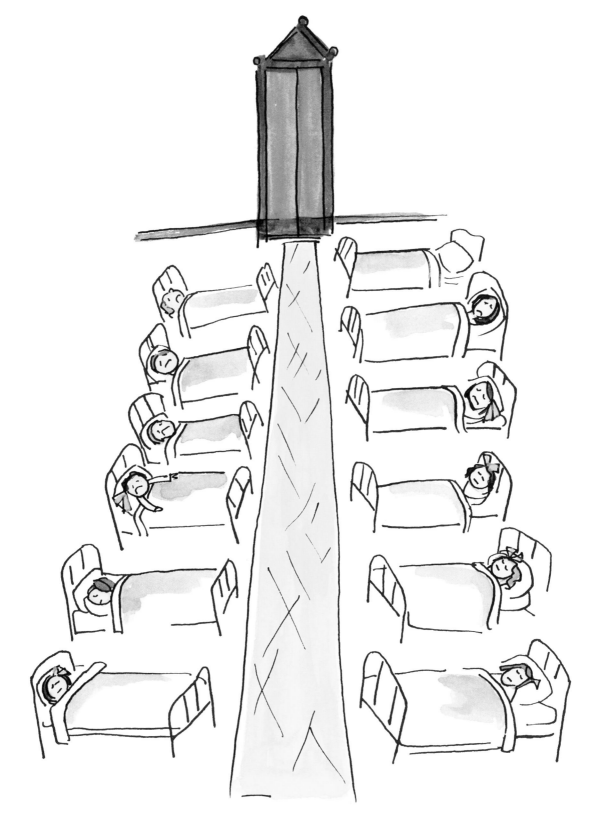

It was the night before Christmas

And all through the house

Not a creature was stirring

Not even the mouse.

For like everyone else in that house which was old
The poor mouse was in bed with a miserable cold.

And only

Our brave little Madeline

Was up and about

And feeling

Just fine.

Suddenly came a knock
Which made her pause—

Could it perhaps be Santa Claus?

But no . . .

A rug merchant was at the door.

He had twelve rugs, he had no more.

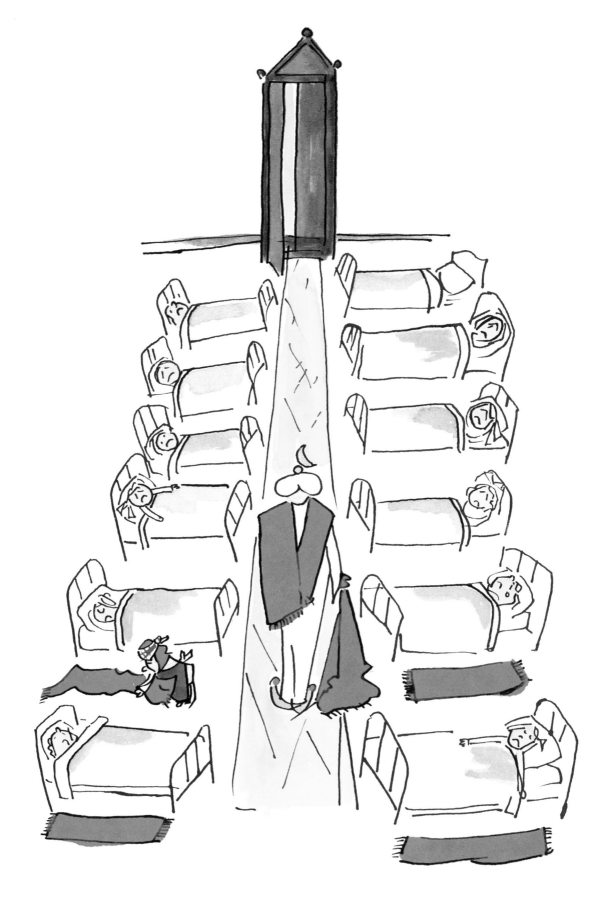

"Why, these," said Madeline, "would be so neat
For our ice-cold in the morning feet."

"It seems to me," said Miss Clavel,

"That you have chosen very well."

And only

Our brave little Madeline

Without the rugs

Which he had sold

The rug merchant got awfully cold.

"To sell my rugs," he cried, "was silly!

Without them I am very chilly."

He wants to get them back—

But will he?

He made it—back to Madeline's door—
He couldn't take one footstep more.

And little Madeline set about
To find a way to thaw him out.

The merchant, who was tall and thin
(And also a ma-gi-ci-an)
Bravely took his medicine.

The magician, as he took his pill,

Said, "Ask me, Madeline, what you will."

Said she, "I've cooked a dinner nutritious.

Will you please help me with these dishes?"

"If you'll clear up
I'll go and see
If I can find
A Christmas tree."

His magic ring he gave a glance
And went into a special trance—
The dirty dishes washed themselves
And jumped right back upon the shelves.

And then he mumbled words profound—

"ABRACADABRA"
BRACADABR
RACADAB
ACADA
CAD
A!"

That made the carpets leave the ground—

And twelve little girls were on their way—

To surprise their parents on Christmas Day.

Miss Clavel again quite well

Thought it time to ring her bell

Which quickly broke the magic spell.

And now we're back, all twelve right here
To wish our friends a HAPPY NEW YEAR!

The Isle of God
(or Madeline's Origin)

With original sketches of Madeline
from Ludwig Bemelmans' notebooks

Ludwig and Madeleine Bemelmans

W hen Barbara was two, we spent the summer on the Île d'Yeu, which lies in the Bay of Biscay, off the west coast of France. I have forgotten why we decided to go there. Most probably somebody told us about it.

The Île d'Yeu is immediately beautiful and at once familiar. Its round, small harbor is stuffed with boats; the big tuna schooners lie in the center; around them are sleek sardine and lobster boats. One can walk around in the harbor over the decks of boats. Only between bows and sterns shine triangles of green water. Twice a day there is a creaking of hulls and a tilting of masts; all the boats begin to settle, to lean on their neighbors; the tide, all the water, runs out of the harbor, and the bottom is dry.

The first house you come to is a small poem of a hotel. It has a bridal suite with a pompom-curtained bed, a chaste washstand, pale pink wallpaper with white pigeons flying over it, and three fauteuils, tangerine velvet and every one large enough for two, closely held, to sit together.

The five-foot proprietor rubs his hands, hops about, glares at employees, smiles at guests. Madame sits behind an ornate desk in the dining-room, her eyes everywhere. The kitchen is bright and smells of good butter, the linen is white, the silver gleams, the waiter is spotless. Outside, under an awning, behind a hedge of well-watered yew trees, overlooking the harbor, are the apéritif tables and chairs.

The prospectus states besides that the hotel has *"eau chaude et froide, chauffage central, tout confort moderne"*—all this is of no consequence, because you can never get a room there. The hotel has but twenty-six rooms, and these are reserved, year after year, by the same people, French families.

Further down is the Hôtel des Voyageurs, sixty rooms, the same thing, the bridal suite in green, the prices somewhat more moderate, the *confort* less *moderne*, but also all booked by April. "Ah, if you would only have written me a letter in March," say the proprietors of both places several times daily from June to September.

Walking down the Quai Sadi-Carnot, you turn right and go through the rue de la Sardine. This street is beautifully named; the houses on both sides touch your shoulders and only a man with one short leg can walk through it in comfort, as half the street is taken up by a sidewalk.

At the end of the Street of the Sardine is the Island's store, the Nouvelles Galeries Insulaires. Its owner Monsieur Penaud will find a place for you to live. Île d'Yeu should really be Île de Dieu, Monsieur Penaud explained, "d'Yeu" being the ancient and faulty way the Islanders spelled "of God." He established us in a fisherman's house, at the holiest address in this world, namely: No. 3, rue du Paradis, Saint-Sauveur, Île d'Yeu.

Our house was a sage, white, well-designed building. Through every door and window of it smiled the marine charm of the Island. The sea was no more than sixty yards from our door. Across the street was an eleventh-century church, whose steeple was built in the shape of a lighthouse. Over the house a brace of gulls hung in the air; there was the murmur of the sea; an old rowboat, with a sailor painted on its keel, stood up in the corner of the garden and served as a chicken coop.

The vegetables in the garden, the fruit on the trees, and the chicken eggs went with the house; included also was a bicycle, trademarked "Hirondelle." It is a nice thing to take over a household so living, complete, and warm, and dig up radishes that someone else has planted for you and cut flowers in a garden that someone else has tended.

The coast of the Island is a succession of small, private beaches, each one like a room, its walls three curtains of rock and greenery. There is a cave to dress in. Once you arrive, it is yours. On the open side is the water, little waves, fine sand; and out on the green ocean all day long the sardine fleet crosses back and forth with colored sails leaning over the water.

There seem to be only three kinds of people: sailors, their hundred-times-patched sensible pants and blouses every shade of color; children; and everywhere two little bent old women dressed in black, their sharp profiles hooked together in gossip. Like crows in a tree they are, and rightly enough, called "*vieux corbeaux*."

Posing everywhere are fish and the things relating to them. The sardine is the banana of the Île d'Yeu: you slip and fall on it. It looks out of the small market baskets that the *vieux corbeaux* carry home; its tail sticks out of fishermen's pockets; it is dragged by in boxes and barrels. Other fish, the tuna predominating, wander by on the shoulders of strong sailors, tied to bicycles, pushed by pairs of boys in carts.

———— ·+·⊰◈⊱·+· ————

One day I bought four lobsters and rode back to the rue du Paradis and almost ran into Paradise itself. Pedaling along with the sack over my shoulder, both hands in my pockets and tracing fancy curves in the roadbed, I came to a bend, which is hidden by some dozen pine trees. Around this turn raced the Island's only automobile, a four-horsepower Super-Rosengart, belonging to the baker of Saint-Sauveur. This car is a fragrant, flour-covered breadbasket on wheels; it threw me in a wide curve off the bicycle into a bramble bush. I took the car's doorhandle off with my elbow.

I asked the baker to take me to the hospital in Saint-Sauveur, but he said that, according to French law, a car must remain exactly where it was when the accident occurred, so that the gendarmes could make their proper deductions and see who was on the wrong side of the road. I tried to change his mind, but he said, "Permit me, *alors*, monsieur, if you use words like that, then it is of no use at all to go on with this conversation."

Having spoken, he went on to pick up his *pain de ménage* and some croissants that were scattered on the road, and then spread aside the branches of the thicket to look for the doorhandle of his Super-Rosengart. I took my lobsters and went to the hospital on foot.

A doctor came, with a cigarette stub hanging out of his lower lip. With a blunt needle he wobbled into my arm. "*Excusez-moi,*" he said, "*mais votre peau est dure!*" I was put into a small white carbolicky bed. In the next room was a little girl who had had her appendix out, and on the ceiling over my bed was a dark crack that, in the varying light of morning, noon, and evening, looked like a rabbit, like the profile of Léon Blum, and at last, in conformity with the Island, like a tremendous sardine.

I saw the nun bringing soup to the little girl. I remembered the stories my mother had told me of life in the convent school at Altötting, and the little girl, the hospital, the room, the crank on the bed, the nurse, the old doctor, who looked like Léon Blum, all fell into place.

I thought about where Madeline and her friends should live and decided on Paris. I made the first sketches on a sidewalk table outside the Restaurant Voltaire on the quai of that same name. The first words of the text, "In an old house in Paris / that was covered with vines," were written on the back of a menu in Pete's Tavern on the corner of Eighteenth Street and Irving Place in New York. *Madeline* was first published in 1939.

It took about ten years to think of the next one, which was *Madeline's Rescue.* One day, after that was finished and in print, I stood and looked down at the Seine opposite Notre Dame. Some little boys were pointing at something floating in the river. One of them shouted: "Ah, there comes the wooden leg of my grandfather." I looked at the object that was approaching and discovered that in my book I had the Seine flowing in the wrong direction.

—Ludwig Bemelmans

HE WAS SURE AND QUICK ON ICE —

ONE NEVER KNOWS HOW A FIESTA ENDS.

ITS TIME
TO TAKE STEP
TO TEACH
A LESSON
TO THAT
BOY PEP

FIRST CAME
SOUP- THEN
FISH THEN
STEAK-Chowlut
SALAD-
ICECREAM
ALMOND CAKE

AND MISS CLAVEL SAID
"ISNT HE NICE"

Barbara, Madeleine, and Ludwig Bemelmans
Bedford Village, New York, 1940

Ludwig and Barbara Bemelmans
Gramercy Park Studio,
New York, 1941